ATTENTION DEFICIT DISORDER

ATTENTION DEFICIT DISORDER

WENDY MORAGNE

The Millbrook Medical
Library

The Millbrook Press
Brookfield, Connecticut

Library of Congress Cataloging–in–Publication Data
Moragne, Wendy.
Attention deficit disorder / Wendy Moragne.
p.   cm.— (The Millbrook medical library)
Includes bibliographical references and index.
Summary: Explains the nature of attention deficit disorder,
the various forms of treatment, and the many challenges
faced by those who live with it.
ISBN 1-56294-674-9 (lib. bdg.)
1. Attention-deficit hyperactivity disorder—Juvenile literature.
[1. Attention-deficit hyperactivity disorder.] I. Title. II. Series.
RJ506.H9M66   1996
618.92'8589—dc20   96-14905 CIP AC

Photographs courtesy of Stock, Boston: pp. 19 (Paul Fortin),
25 (Jean-Claude LeJeune), 35 (Judy Gelles), 41 (Michael Dwyer),
49 (Rhoda Sidney), 52 (Frank Siteman), 64 (Jean-Claude LeJeune),
69 (Elizabeth Crews), 76 (James Carroll), 81 (Michael Dwyer),
86 (Richard Pasley), 95 (Richard Pasley).

Published by The Millbrook Press, Inc.
Brookfield, Connecticut
Copyright ©1996 by Wendy Moragne
All rights reserved
5 4 3 2 1

To the young people and adults with ADD and their families, who so willingly shared their stories with me, and to my family, who gave me so much support.

Contents

ATTENTION DEFICIT DISORDER

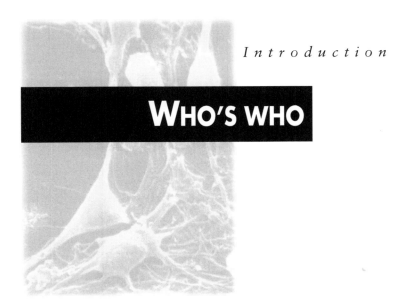

WHO'S WHO

In this book, you will read the stories of eleven coura-geous and thoughtful young people who rose to the chal-lenges posed by a chronic disorder called attention deficit disorder, or ADD. These young people describe what it is like to cope with this lifelong condition during adoles-cence, with all of the personal and social demands that arise during this time of life. You will find out how they learned to succeed, despite their problems. They hope their experiences will inspire as well as teach you.

Brian, 15 years old
Brian began having problems at home when he was six years old, and at school when he was seven. He had difficul-ty keeping his hands to himself, often displaying aggressive and impulsive behavior. After upsets in his family life and suspension from school on several occasions, Brian was evaluated by a psychologist and diagnosed with ADD at the age of nine. The use of behavior-management techniques and medication have helped Brian with his problems.

Michael, 12 years old
Michael displayed impulsive, daredevil behavior from the time he was eleven months old, when he learned to climb out of his crib. This behavior continued until Michael was seven years old, when his family sought help from a qualified psychologist who diagnosed him as having ADD. Michael began a course of treatment that included following a behavior-management program and taking medication.

Evan, 10 years old
For many years, Evan's temper tantrums and aggressive behavior embarrassed his older brother and frightened his younger sister. His parents sought help for him just after his eighth birthday. Two years later, after receiving treatment, Evan is better able to control his behavior, although he still sometimes displays hyperactive and aggressive behavior.

Jeremy, 17 years old
Jeremy took the blame for all of the arguments he had with his younger sister, Jessica, even though Jessica was often the instigator. Jeremy's parents always assumed that Jeremy was the culprit simply because of his long history of behavior problems. At school, both his teachers and his peers criticized and ridiculed him for his behavior problems and lack of focus. Even after receiving a diagnosis of ADD and benefitting from treatment, Jeremy continued to suffer from low self-esteem. When he reached high school, however, he discovered a love and talent for horticulture. This achievement has helped him feel better about himself, encouraging him to strive for success in other areas of his life as well.

Steven, 18 years old
During his early school years, Steven's problems with concentration prevented him from completing assignments on time and from meeting other responsibilities. He received

constant criticism from his parents and teachers, and was often accused of being lazy and of not trying hard enough. Now ready to start college, Steven feels he has made steady progress since being diagnosed with ADD at the age of eleven and receiving treatment.

Sara, 17 years old

Before receiving treatment for ADD at the age of sixteen, Sara found it difficult to finish school assignments or complete chores around the house. She also found it almost impossible to meet her curfew, which caused problems between her and her mother. Sara eventually dropped out of school and became involved with the wrong crowd. Fortunately, Sara's mother was able to get help for her daughter from a psychiatrist, who diagnosed Sara with ADD and prescribed medication and regular counseling for her. Although Sara's relationship with her mother is still sometimes strained, it is much improved, as is Sara's self-esteem and self-confidence.

Julie, 15 years old

Julie struggled with both her schoolwork and her social skills throughout much of her childhood. Because of Julie's daydreaming and inability to concentrate, Julie's mother had to tutor Julie at home to help her keep up at school. Because of Julie's self-consciousness and need for constant reassurance, her mother took her to a psychologist when Julie was twelve years old. The doctor diagnosed her with ADD, which he believed to be responsible for much of her problem with concentration and focus. He also told her that she had an anxiety disorder. With treatment, Julie is finally learning to make friends and explore her talents.

Ben, 13 years old

Ben was a mischievous toddler and a hyperactive first grader. In second grade, a serious reading problem surfaced, and Ben started to fall behind his classmates. When a psychologist evaluated Ben at the age of eight, she found that he had both ADD and a condition called dyslexia. With the help of medication for his ADD symptoms and special reading instruction for his dyslexia, Ben is coping much better today.

Mark, 14 years old
Mark knew he was not stupid, but school was a struggle for him, nonetheless. He could not sit still and he constantly made mistakes on his written assignments. He received much criticism from his teacher, and his classmates teased him regularly. After a psychologist diagnosed him as having ADD, Mark started taking Ritalin and his parents worked with behavior-management techniques to help him improve his behavior. Today Mark is on the honor roll in middle school.

Beth, 13 years old
Throughout most of her childhood, Beth found it impossible to take and meet daily responsibilities at home and at school. In addition to being messy and disorganized, Beth also seemed unable to follow through on completing chores around the house. Her older sister, Allison, not only resented having to pick up after Beth, but was also jealous of all the attention Beth received from their parents, even though the attention was mostly negative. After Beth was diagnosed with ADD at the age of ten, her sister became more understanding of her and showed more patience toward her. A turning point for Beth occurred when she was twelve and her parents allowed her to adopt a kitten. She successfully nurtured her pet, proving to herself and to her family that she could accept and meet responsibilities. Her success helped boost her self-esteem.

Holly, 16 years old
Holly's sisters, Becky and Cindy, often argued with Holly about her impulsive and inattentive behavior. The constant

fighting led their parents to seek help from a psychologist, who diagnosed Holly with ADD. Through family therapy and a behavior-management program set up for all three girls, family life has improved. Now in high school, Holly has been able to earn higher grades and make new friends, which has enabled her to feel a sense of self-worth and self-confidence. This increased self-esteem has also helped improve her relationships with her sisters and parents.

WHAT IS ATTENTION DEFICIT DISORDER?

BRIAN'S STORY

As a young child, Brian's easygoing nature and sharp mind delighted other people. Even his little sisters, Elaine (two years younger) and Lori (four years younger), considered him a fun and playful older brother. But as he matured, Brian began to have difficulties, especially with Lori. He pulled her hair, pinched her cheek, and broke her toys. He did anything to annoy and pester her, and although he did not want to hurt her, he could not stop, no matter how hard he tried.

Brian's parents constantly scolded him. "Keep your hands to yourself or you'll be punished," they warned. It seemed that school was the only place where Brian was able to avoid getting into trouble. Unfortunately, school, too, presented a problem for Brian when he entered second grade. After only a few weeks, Brian was already behind in his *work. Unlike most of his classmates, Brian could finish only half an assignment by the time the teacher collected the papers, and he often had to stay in at recess to complete his work.*

"One day while I was in at recess trying to do my work, I was distracted by the noise of a bull-dozer off in the distance," recalls Brian. "I knew I was supposed to be doing my work, but I just kept hearing the low hum of the bulldozer and I couldn't keep my mind on what I was doing. I kept thinking about the bulldozer. Since I couldn't see it, I was wondering if it was clearing land for houses to be built or if it was pushing dirt into place, like at a landfill or something. I couldn't stop wondering and imagining what kind of work the bulldozer was doing. I never did complete my school assignment, and my teacher sent a note home to my parents. I got punished. I loved to play computer games and I wasn't allowed to use the computer for two days."

Brian's problems at school worsened as the school year progressed. He found it difficult to keep from bothering other children during class. He poked and prodded at them with his fingers, his pencil, and even his feet. Annoyed, Brian's classmates began to slide their desks away from him, and they rarely asked him to join their play-ground activities at recess. These rejections hurt Brian's feelings and made him angry with both his classmates and himself. He knew what the other children did not like about his behavior, but he could not seem to control himself. Frustrated and lonely, Brian began to think of himself as a bad person.

At home after school, Brian found that the only children who wanted to play with him were

People with ADD often find it difficult to concentrate and are easily distracted by noises, activites, or their daydreams.

all two or three years younger than he. Because Brian was older and stronger, the younger children allowed him to set up the rules of the games and to take charge. One day Brian convinced a five-year-old friend to climb a tree with him. The friend climbed to the lowest branch and stopped there, realizing that he might fall if he went higher. Brian, on the other hand, never thought about what might happen if he were to climb higher, and before long, had climbed almost to the top. A branch suddenly snapped and Brian fell to the ground, breaking his arm.

By the end of second grade, Brian was behind in all his subjects. His teacher called his parents in for a special conference and discussed having Brian repeat second grade. Brian's parents knew that their son was bright, and they did not want to see him held back. After much discussion, they persuaded the teacher to pass him to third grade under the condition that Brian attend summer school in order to catch up to his classmates. It was a summer Brian would never forget.

"My grandparents have a house at the beach," says Brian. "Every summer we spend a few weeks at their place. Because of summer school, we were able to go only for a weekend. I was so angry that I punched everything in sight when I came home from summer school each day. Then my mom punished me. That summer was really horrible."

When Brian began third grade in the fall, he faced new problems. During the second week of school, his teacher sent him to the principal's office for knocking down a classmate in the cafeteria line. The following week, Brian missed recess three times because he failed to complete his math assignments during class time. When he was allowed to go to recess, he ended up in fist fights with his classmates. His problems with aggression worsened to the point where he eventually got suspended from school.

At home, Brian continued to torment Lori, who had grown afraid of him. Brian also often found it impossible to concentrate long enough to finish his homework assignments, and when he did complete his work, he usually forgot to take it back to school the following day.

"I found myself screaming and yelling and punishing every day," says Brian's mother. "I was beginning to feel like a real failure as a mother. I would talk to some other mothers with children Brian's age, and they were not going through what we were. My son was always the one having the problems. I tried to hold my temper, but I was so exhausted from fighting and worrying that it did no good. I also felt guilty about punishing Brian all the time. And I felt guilty about always telling Brian's sisters to be quiet and good so that I could deal with Brian. My husband and I were spending all of our time and effort on Brian. I felt so miserable and depressed."

"Mom was a basket case," recalls Brian's sister Elaine. "I didn't really understand what was happening to our family. I was seven. Lori was five. Mom yelled and screamed a lot. And she cried a lot, too. I felt sorry for her. I knew that she was upset with Brian all the time. I was upset with him, too. I was beginning not to like him. I knew I was supposed to like him because he was my big brother, but I hated the way he always upset our family. I sometimes wished he would just disappear."

In the spring, just after Brian's ninth birthday, Brian and his mother went to see a psychologist named Dr. Sanders. Dr. Sanders gave Brian tests and talked for a long time with him and his mother. He asked to speak with Brian's father and sisters later that week, and he also phoned Brian's teacher. From his evaluation, Dr. Sanders concluded that Brian's problems resulted from attention deficit disorder, or ADD.

Dr. Sanders arranged for another doctor to examine Brian to determine whether he could take medication known to help people with ADD manage their symptoms. Brian's doctor prescribed a medication called Ritalin for Brian to take twice every day. Brian did not mind taking the medication. He found that it was not much different from taking vitamin pills.

Dr. Sanders set up a behavior-management program for Brian and his family and asked that they all meet with him every other week in order to monitor their progress. The behavior-management program that Dr. Sanders set up helped Brian work on controlling his temper and keeping his hands to himself.

Brian finished the school year with good grades and compliments on his progress from his teacher. Without question, he could move on to fourth grade. Brian had many reasons to feel better about himself that spring. Some of his classmates had begun to spend time with him, and they had included him in a few games at recess. A classmate even invited Brian to an end-of-the-year party, which really boosted his self-esteem.

Since Brian's diagnosis, Brian's mother also has been diagnosed with ADD. She takes Ritalin to help her manage her symptoms. "Much of the trouble I was having in trying to cope with Brian before his diagnosis and treatment stemmed from

*the fact that I, too, had ADD, but didn't know it,"
says Brian's mother. "I feel much better about
myself now, and I feel that I can relate to Brian
much better, too."*

*Brian is now fifteen and in high school. He is
doing well both at home and at school. The combined use of medication, behavior-management
techniques, and family therapy has made a dramat-
ic improvement in the lives of Brian and his family.
Brian has great plans for the future. "I want to be
a famous writer and movie producer someday," he
explains. "I love to write, and I hope to be able to
write my own movie scripts and then produce the
movies. That's my big dream. I really enjoy science
fiction, so the plot will probably be something
unusual, something related to science fiction."*

*"Brian has turned out to be a neat big brother
after all," says Elaine. "The family therapy has
helped all of us. We understand that Brian couldn't
help the way he was acting. Now that he is on the
medication and receiving counseling from Dr.
Sanders, things are much better. He has learned to
control himself more, and we have learned how to
relate to him. Not every day is perfect, but most are
pretty good. I never wish for Brian to disappear
anymore!"*

UNDERSTANDING ADD

Because of the symptoms associated with ADD, many people mistakenly think that children with ADD are spoiled,
immature, or lacking in manners, or that they come from
bad homes where their parents do not care about them or
do not exercise discipline. In fact, ADD is believed to be
the result of a problem over which children and adults
with the disorder have no control. Current research indi-

cates that the brain chemistry of people with ADD may be different from that of people without ADD. Experts believe that, as a result of this difference, people with ADD tend to have difficulty paying attention, thinking before acting, or sitting still.

Who Has ADD?

Attention deficit disorder affects males and females, children and adults, and people of all races. ADD can run in families, passed from one generation to another. If you were to study the family history of a person with ADD, you would probably find other members of the family—a parent, sibling, grandparent, or cousin—who also showed signs of having ADD. Not everyone with ADD is evaluated by a professional, however, so many people may not know the history of the disorder in their families.

CURRENT RESEARCH INDICATES THAT THE BRAIN CHEMISTRY OF PEOPLE WITH ADD MAY BE DIFFERENT FROM THAT OF PEOPLE WITHOUT ADD.

An estimated 3 to 5 percent of children in the United States have ADD—about two million young people. Some of the symptoms of ADD tend to diminish as the child matures into adulthood, while others may be present throughout a person's life.

What Are the Symptoms?

No two people with ADD experience the disorder in exactly the same way. Some suffer from so many symptoms associated with the disorder that several aspects of their lives are affected. Other people experience only a few symptoms, which occur when they are trying to complete schoolwork or chores at home.

In general, the more symptoms a person has, the more

Impulsive, and often dangerous, behavior is frequent in people with ADD, who sometimes act without thinking of the consequences.

noticeable it will be that he or she has a problem, and the more quickly he or she will receive proper treatment. Individuals who experience very few symptoms or who compensate for their symptoms particularly well may never be diagnosed and treated. Others, like Brian, who experience obvious difficulties at home with family members and at school with assignments and classmates, are more likely to be diagnosed and treated.

ABOUT 3 TO 5 PERCENT OF THE POPULATION OF CHILDREN IN THE UNITED STATES HAVE ADD. ATTENTION DEFICIT DISORDER AFFECTS BOTH MALES AND FEMALES IN ALL AGE GROUPS AND FROM ALL ETHNIC BACKGROUNDS.

Many individuals with ADD find it difficult to concentrate on and stick with a task, especially when it is unvaried. A whole worksheet of math problems, for example, may seem monotonous for some students. A student without ADD is likely to complete the tedious assignment, while a student with ADD is likely to become sidetracked and not complete the work.

It is common for young people with ADD to act impulsively. They tend to act before they have thought about the consequences of their actions. For example, Brian acted impulsively when he tormented his sister and when he climbed too high in the tree. Because these young people do not think ahead, they often find themselves in dangerous situations and are more likely to get hurt, as Brian did.

Another characteristic of some young people with ADD is that they are overactive, or hyperactive. They tend to be more fidgety and restless than other young people, especially in situations in which they are expected to sit still or to be quiet, such as in the classroom. Some are also physically aggressive. It is extremely difficult for these people to keep their hands to themselves, and they often have angry outbursts during which they may hit or push others. At home, Brian constantly pinched Lori and pulled her hair, and at school, he pestered his classmates and got into fist fights.

In addition to having ADD, some young people may also have difficulty learning subjects such as reading, spelling, or math. Research indicates that almost one third of the young people with ADD also have difficulty learning, which makes success in school even tougher for these students.

TYPES OF TREATMENT

Several medications have proven helpful in treating ADD, including stimulants, which seem to compensate for the difference in the brain chemistry that causes problems for people with ADD. Tricyclic antidepressants, used in treating depression, and clonidine, a high-blood-pressure medication, are also useful in alleviating symptoms of ADD.

As effective as medication can be, it is not likely to solve all of the problems caused by ADD. The most successful approach to treating ADD tends to be the use of medication combined with behavior management and counseling. Young people with ADD benefit most when medical professionals, parents, and teachers work as a team to help them stay focused and successfully complete assignments or chores. With help, these young people can learn how to take responsibility for their actions and achieve goals both at home and at school.

Attention deficit disorder is a condition that can affect a person's entire life. It can also affect a person's feelings about himself or herself. Although ADD is not curable, much is being done to help children and adults with the disorder. With proper treatment, it is possible for people with ADD to live happy, prosperous lives.

Chapter 2 may help you to recognize some of the symptoms of ADD in yourself or in someone you know.

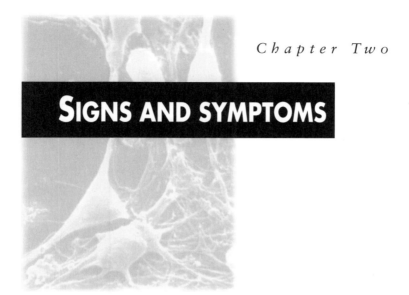

SIGNS AND SYMPTOMS

Health professionals consider the types of behaviors listed below as symptoms of ADD. The behaviors that characterize ADD fall into three main categories: inattention, impulsiveness, and hyperactivity. In other words, people with ADD are likely to have difficulty paying attention (inattention), thinking before acting (impulsiveness), and sitting still (hyperactivity).

CHARACTERISTIC SYMPTOMS OF ADD

To be diagnosed as having ADD, a person must be carefully examined and evaluated by qualified, experienced professionals. A psychologist or other health professional must find that this person has exhibited at least six of the nine behaviors in either of the categories listed below. Additionally, the behavior must have begun before the person was age seven and must have persisted for at least six months.

Inattention

A person who has ADD may show these symptoms of inattention:

1. often fails to give close attention to details or makes careless mistakes in schoolwork or other activities
2. often has difficulty paying attention during tasks or play activities
3. often seems not to be listening when spoken to directly
4. often does not follow through on instructions and fails to finish schoolwork or chores
5. often has difficulty organizing tasks and activities
6. often avoids, dislikes, or is reluctant to do school work or homework
7. often loses things, such as toys, schoolwork, pencils, or books
8. often is easily distracted by what is going on in the immediate environment
9. often is forgetful in daily activities

Impulsiveness and Hyperactivity

A person who has ADD may show these symptoms of impulsiveness and hyperactivity:

1. often fidgets with hands or feet, or squirms in seat
2. often leaves seat in classroom or other places where remaining seated is required
3. often runs or climbs in situations in which it is inappropriate. Adolescents may feel restless
4. often has difficulty playing or working quietly
5. often is "on the go" or acts as if "driven by a motor"
6. often talks excessively
7. often blurts out answers before questions have been completed
8. often has difficulty awaiting turn

9. often interrupts or intrudes on others during conversations, games, or other activities

THE VARIED SIGNS

The symptoms of ADD appear during childhood and may continue to present challenges throughout a person's life. Because every individual with ADD is different, not all people show the same signs of the various symptoms. One person might sit quietly, daydreaming. Another might climb to the top of the jungle gym and then stand up. A third might be easily distracted by noise or movement outside the classroom, making it difficult for him or her to learn in school. In addition, at each stage of a person's life, the symptoms may express themselves in different ways.

Michael as an Infant and Toddler

Children sometimes show signs of ADD even before they are born. Michael's mother remembers, "Michael didn't just move around in my stomach, he did somersaults like a gymnast, he kicked like a football punter, and he punched like a boxer! I was absolutely certain I was going to give birth to a great athlete!"

As infants, some children with ADD are very fussy and overly sensitive to touch. Instead of being comforted by their mothers' rocking or patting, the activity disturbs them. They may cry even harder and try to pull away. When they play, they often wander from toy to toy, unable to become interested in any one toy for more than a very short time. Before their first birthday, many babies with ADD can walk or even run. Many are able to climb out of their cribs. Michael's dad reports that his son could climb out of the crib at the age of eleven months.

Michael's mother and I couldn't believe it when early one morning we heard the pitter-patter of lit-

31

tle feet running across the wooden floor of Michael's room. I got there just in time to see Michael heading for the staircase. I checked the crib to see if we had forgotten to pull up the side the night before, but it was up. The next morning, I set my alarm and got up before Michael so that I

THE BEHAVIORS THAT CHARACTERIZE ATTENTION DEFICIT DISORDER FALL INTO THREE MAIN CATEGORIES: INATTENTION, IMPULSIVENESS, AND HYPERACTIVITY. TO BE DIAGNOSED AS HAVING ADD, A PERSON MUST BE CAREFULLY EXAMINED AND EVALUATED BY QUALIFIED, EXPERIENCED PROFESSIONALS.

could see how he managed to get out of the crib. I couldn't believe what I saw. He was able to climb onto the side of the crib and teeter back and forth until his weight shifted toward the outside of the crib. As his body fell toward the floor, he was able to grab onto the sides of the crib and hang like a monkey. Then he would let go and drop to the floor. He did all of this in a matter of seconds. We ended up having to put the crib mattress on the floor and turn the crib upside down over the mattress at night. This was the only way we could keep Michael safe.

Toddlers with ADD often have mood swings, become easily frustrated, and show very little self-control. Some learn to walk and talk early, while others have delayed speech development. Some are very curious. When Michael was two years old, he did something that his parents will always remember.

We had a lock near the top of the front door of our house so that we wouldn't have to worry if Michael awakened before we did in the morning," explains Michael's mother. *"He loved to ride his tricycle, and we were afraid he would leave the house and we wouldn't know it. With the lock beyond his reach, we had peace of mind. But one morning, Michael was nowhere around. To our horror, we found him riding his tricycle down the driveway and into the street. Luckily, it was barely sunup and there was no traffic on the street. We discovered that Michael had dragged a chair over to the door and had unlocked the lock.*

Evan as a Preschooler

Because children with ADD often have difficulty getting along with other children, they are likely to face special difficulties when they enter preschool or kindergarten. Unable to wait their turn, they may push friends off the slide or insist on going first in every game. They may act bossy and decide what games to play. Often if their playmates do not follow their rules, they quit. These children may not be able to follow the teacher's instructions or sit still in class. Nothing may hold their attention for very long. They are likely to interrupt constantly during story time, talk loudly, or run around the room.

Because of problems with hyperactivity and impulsiveness, these children may throw temper tantrums when things do not go their way or when they do not get what they want when they want it. They may break toys or take them apart and then fail to put them back together. In the middle of one activity, they are likely to drop it and go on to another. Their parents often must hover over them to get them to do chores and to complete activities.

"My husband and I bought Evan a beautiful remote-controlled car for his fifth birthday," recalls Evan's grandmother. "This is what he wanted. We spent a lot of money on it, and I just assumed that he would take care of it. His parents had a little family birthday party for him, and by the end of the evening, we were shocked to find that the motor control was no longer working and Evan had the car all pulled apart."

Jeremy and Steven in Elementary School

Some young people with ADD do not experience any serious difficulties until they reach third or fourth grade, when more concentration and discipline are necessary. Those who are hyperactive will often have great difficulty sitting still in class. They may find excuses for leaving their seats, such as making frequent trips to the pencil sharpener, bathroom, or water fountain.

Jeremy had always been a hyperactive child, but by the time he was ten years old, his behavior was so disruptive at school that his parents sought help for him. "I couldn't sit still," recalls Jeremy. "I used to slide off of the edge of my chair or hang over my desk—anything to get out of my seat. If I could get away with going to the bathroom a hundred times during the school day, I would. My teachers were always calling my parents about my fidgety behavior. My parents finally took me to a neurologist to see what was wrong with me, and that's when I was diagnosed with ADD. The doctor put me on a medicine called Dexedrine, and it helped a lot."

Impulsiveness presents a problem for many young people with ADD. In class they often blurt out answers without first being called on by the teacher. They find it difficult to wait their turn in line in the lunchroom or elsewhere, and they may push and shove their way to the front of the line. Because they are unable to plan ahead, these young people usually do their work in a disorganized fashion. They tend to do their schoolwork and chores in a hurry and, as a result, make careless errors. Their bedrooms are likely to be messy, which makes

It's often difficult for a person with ADD to concentrate for long periods and to organize their books and papers, which makes schoolwork especially challenging for them.

it hard for them to find books, homework papers, or clothing.

Many young people with ADD find it especially difficult to pay attention or to stick with a task for long periods of time because they become easily distracted by their own thoughts as well as by the noises and activities around them. As a result, they often have difficulty completing assignments or doing so on time. This is especially true when they are working on repetitious school assignments, or when performing a task that does not interest them. On the other hand, many young people with ADD have no problem concentrating and sticking with a project if it is something they enjoy or is something they have chosen to do. For example, Jeremy was often unable to finish his homework because he became too distracted, but he had no trouble sitting for hours playing computer games.

> **MANY YOUNG PEOPLE WITH ADD ALSO HAVE LEARNING OR BEHAVIOR PROBLEMS, WHICH CAN MAKE LIFE EVEN MORE CHALLENGING FOR THEM.**

"I hated spelling and math, and I could only sit still long enough to read a little at a time," says Jeremy. "My grades were never very good, and my parents always seemed disappointed when I brought home my report cards. The only things that really held my attention were television and computer games."

Young people with ADD are often described as immature because their behavior seems to be like that of someone three or four years younger. They may have difficulty remembering rules, and they usually do not tolerate frustration well. Feelings of frustration are likely to lead to temper outbursts. Many of these young people have special difficulties coping with changes in routine.

Steven recalls a typical school day before he began treatment for ADD at the age of eleven.

My mom would wake me up at seven o'clock. The bus would come at seven forty-five, and I was late every day. The trouble always started when I was trying to get dressed because I would always end up doing something else instead. I love football, and sometimes I would just sit on my bed and look through my football cards. I would forget all about getting ready for school. The next thing I knew, my mom would be screaming that the bus was at the corner. Half the time, I would get to school and realize that I had left my books or my homework at home. My mom would have to drive them over to the school for me. Then she would be really angry.

At school, I had trouble finishing my work. When I did finish it, my teacher would return it with red marks all over it. My teacher always said that she knew I could do better and she didn't know why I always made so many mistakes. I felt bad when she said this to me, especially since she always said it out loud in front of the whole class. At recess, the other kids didn't want to hang around with me. They teased me and called me names. They would make me so mad that I would get into fist fights with them. Then I would get punished, like lose recess the next day or have to go to the principal's office.

After school, I would have so much trouble concentrating that it would take me forever to finish my homework. I wasn't allowed to watch television until it was finished, and I usually ended up missing my favorite shows. Sometimes I felt so angry that I would take all of my books and papers and throw them on the floor.

Sara as a Teenager

The teen years present new challenges for young people with ADD. Adolescence is a time of intense growth and change. During this period, a young person progresses from childhood to adulthood—physically, emotionally, and socially. It is often a bumpy road, filled with emotional upsets, feelings of insecurity, and a desire to be independent. At home, teenagers want their parents and siblings to treat them more like grownups than like children. At school, their self-esteem depends a great deal on what their classmates think of them. They want to feel liked and accepted. At the same time, their schoolwork and homework assignments become more complex. They also have many different teachers, one for each subject, and they must change classrooms several times during the day. Although the teen years are tough for everyone, they may be especially difficult for young people with ADD.

Like their younger counterparts, teenagers with ADD tend to be restless, to have difficulty concentrating, and to do things without thinking about the consequences. At home they are more likely to get into arguments with their parents over how late they stay out or over how they spend time with their friends. They are more likely to have run-ins with authority figures, and they tend to be involved in more auto accidents than other teens. At school, these students are often behind in their work, which is likely to leave them feeling frustrated and, as a result, more likely to cut class or drop out of school than other teens.

Teenagers with ADD often feel upset and frustrated about not fitting in, about not accomplishing goals, and about being constantly criticized or punished. The failure that these teens experience leave many of them feeling worthless or hopeless, and some even experiment with alcohol or drugs in an attempt to feel better.

"I was always getting punished," says Sara, an eleventh-grader. "At home, my room was a mess and my mom would always be yelling at me to clean it up. Or she would yell at me for not helping around the house. I would try, but I just couldn't ever seem to do it. And I would miss my curfew all the time. Then my mom would punish me, like take away television or ground me. I hated myself for getting punished all the time. And, truthfully, I even hated my mom for giving me so many punishments. We always ended up in arguments, which just made everything worse."

On the bright side, many teenagers find that some of their ADD symptoms diminish during adolescence as they mature into adulthood. Those who suffer from hyperactivity are especially likely to see this symptom diminish as they age.

OTHER RELATED CHALLENGES

Many young people with ADD have additional learning or behavior problems, which can make life even more challenging for them. The associated problems should be treated as seriously as the attention deficit disorder. Health professionals and educational professionals can help in the diagnosis and treatment of these problems.

Learning Difficulties
Almost one third of all children with ADD also have a learning difficulty, which makes it harder for them to read, spell, or do math. Dyslexia—a language-communication disorder that affects a person's ability to read, write, spell, and/or speak—is one of the most common of these associated conditions. Learning difficulties add to the hardships students with ADD face in school because they make it even tougher for these students to complete their school assignments and to do so correctly and on time.

Speech and Language Difficulties
As children grow older, they are usually able to rely on words rather than actions to express their needs. For children with ADD who also have a problem with speech and

language development, however, it is often difficult or even impossible for them to express themselves. These children often resort to actions rather than words to express their needs or desires. For example, a child with ADD who also has a limited vocabulary and poor grammar may hit or shove to get a toy away from another child rather than simply ask for it.

The behavior of very young children is controlled by the language of older people. For example, a parent will say "no, no" when a toddler misbehaves. As children grow older, however, they must learn to control their own behavior, without someone else telling them what to do. They need to remember rules—to actually hear them inside their heads—in order to behave properly.

Unfortunately, young people with ADD who have an associated speech or language difficulty may have trouble using language for self-control. One type of therapy, called cognitive-behavioral self-control therapy (CBT), teaches these individuals to talk to themselves as a way of controlling their behavior. This technique, which works best for children seven to eleven years old, can be taught by a professional, such as a psychologist or speech therapist. As part of this therapy, young people learn to:

- recognize when they are having a problem, stop the action, and take time to think about the problem and how it can be solved

- figure out what is causing the problem

- come up with possible solutions to the problem and evaluate each one

- choose the best solution and try it

Motor Coordination Problems
Motor coordination—the ability to manage complex movements with hands, fingers, and feet—may be a problem for some young people with ADD. These individuals

Sports and other physical activities require coordination of hands, fingers, and feet, which people with ADD are often lacking.

seem to be clumsy or uncoordinated when writing with a pencil, throwing a ball, or jumping rope, for example. Because there is often much emphasis on sports for males, boys with this problem may also have social and self-esteem problems because of their difficulties in this area.

Oppositional Defiant Disorder
Young people with the psychological condition known as oppositional defiant disorder tend to be stubborn, aggressive, and disobedient. They are usually quick to lose their temper, and they tend to blame others for their mistakes. In addition, they are likely to appear angry and resentful, and they often break rules just for spite.

Conduct Disorder
Another related psychological problem is called conduct disorder. Individuals with conduct disorder seem not to care about the basic rights of other people. They are often aggressive, cruel, and physically violent. During the teen years, these people often have problems with alcohol and drug use. Fortunately, for many, the problems diminish as they reach adulthood. For others, however, the difficulties continue and may lead to more serious problems.

Mood Disorder
Young people with mood disorder often have trouble sleeping. They may have difficulty falling asleep or may awaken often during the night. They feel tired and bored much of the time and often feel worthless. These individuals may also have frequent changes in eating habits, and often complain of headaches and stomachaches. Some feel depressed and sad; others feel grouchy or on edge.

Anxiety Disorder
Young people with anxiety disorder often suffer from self-consciousness and need excessive reassurance. They may

avoid being alone and may be afraid to be apart from their parents, even during the school day.

When Julie was diagnosed with ADD at the age of twelve, she also found out that she suffered from anxiety disorder. "When I was with my mom, I felt like everything would be okay," says Julie. "When I was by myself, I felt that things were bound to go wrong. I always thought that people didn't like me. I worried that they thought I was different or strange. I didn't have any friends."

There are many ways in which individuals experience the symptoms of ADD. Fortunately, there are also many ways for individuals to cope with those various symptoms and to live happy and successful lives.

Chapter Three

DIAGNOSIS AND TREATMENT

BEN'S STORY

Ben was eight years old when a psychologist named Dr. Miller diagnosed him with ADD. Ben had been exhibiting behavior problems since he was a toddler. At the age of three, he climbed the counters in the kitchen and teetered along the edge. He also managed to climb his swing set and sit on top of it. At the age of five, when Ben started kindergarten, he found it difficult to stay seated or to keep his hands to himself. He poked and grabbed the children around him. It was almost impossible for him to write the letters of the alphabet or spell his name. His handwriting looked like scribble, and he wrote many letters backward. Ben's temper flared when he was teased about this by his classmates, and Ben would punch and kick them.

By the time Ben reached second grade, he had more problems. He found it difficult to read, often becoming distracted by everything else going on around him. He also had trouble recognizing some letters and words. He often confused "b" with "d" and "saw" with "was." There were some simple words that he did not recognize at all. Ben also had a new baby brother at home. Ben's behavior was so rough that his parents could not leave him alone with the baby. Ben seemed to love his brother, but every time he touched him, he hurt him.

In the spring, Ben joined the softball team in town. Ben's dad bought him a new glove and every evening helped him practice throwing and catching. Things went smoothly until Ben's team played their first game against another team. Ben became overly excited, constantly running up to the diamond and shouting. Although he was shouting words of encouragement, he nevertheless annoyed and distracted his teammates. That evening, the coach phoned Ben's parents and told them Ben's behavior was disruptive and unacceptable. This was the turning point for Ben's parents, and they decided to take Ben to see Dr. Miller.

Dr. Miller first spoke with Ben's parents and asked them many questions about Ben's day-to-day behavior. She wanted to get as clear a picture of Ben as possible. Ben's parents explained to Dr. Miller their son's problems with his schoolwork and some of the problems he was having outside of school, such as his behavior with his baby brother and at the softball game.

Dr. Miller then met with Ben. She asked him some questions and gave him written exercises to find out whether he worried a lot or felt anxious in his day-to-day life. Dr. Miller then conducted tests on Ben to determine:

- *his thinking abilities, to measure his intelligence*

- *his academic performance, such as his ability in reading, spelling, and math*

- *how he got along with his friends and family*

- *how he felt about himself and others*

- *his use of his hands and feet, as well as his use of words in daily experiences*

- *the length of time he was able to pay attention*

- *how impulsive he was*

Some of what Dr. Miller asked Ben to do seemed like schoolwork to him. Other things reminded him of drawing and doing puzzles.

Before Dr. Miller made her final diagnosis, she phoned Ben's teacher and asked her questions about Ben's behavior and performance at school. She also arranged for Ben to have a physical examination by his pediatrician to be sure there were no other problems contributing to his difficulties.

When Dr. Miller compiled all of the information she had gathered, she determined that Ben had ADD. In addition, she suspected that he had a problem with reading and writing called dyslexia. Later, Dr. Miller tested Ben for dyslexia and confirmed her suspicions that he had this condition.

Ben's pediatrician prescribed the drug Ritalin to manage Ben's ADD symptoms. Ben and his parents continued to meet with Dr. Miller, the psychologist, on a regular basis and discussed ways to help Ben change his behavior. At school, Ben received individual instruction in reading by a teacher experienced in helping children with dyslexia.

THE DIAGNOSIS

The first step in the treatment of ADD involves obtaining a proper diagnosis from a trained health professional. Pediatricians, neurologists, psychiatrists, psychologists, and social workers are all qualified to evaluate a person who may have ADD. Before completing the diagnosis, the professional may refer the person to other specialists as well. For example, a psychologist might refer a patient to a neurologist in order to determine whether or not there is disease within the nervous system.

The evaluation process for ADD must be thorough and must include a complete family history, interviews with family members and teachers, psychological tests, and a medical examination. Unless the health professional has put together all the information from these various sources, he or she cannot make an accurate diagnosis.

Young people diagnosed with ADD may have different feelings about their condition. Some may feel confused because they do not understand what ADD is or what to expect. Others may use ADD as an excuse to display inappropriate behavior, even after their ability to control it increases with effective treatment. For the most part, however, young people diagnosed with ADD feel a great sense of relief. Finally, they have received an explanation for why they have had so much trouble paying attention at school or why they have not been able to follow rules or get along with their friends, no matter how hard they have tried.

Parents, too, experience a range of emotions after learning their child has ADD. Some feel guilty, mistakenly believing that they did something to cause the condition or that they could have done something to prevent it. Others feel depressed or fearful and worry about their child's future success and happiness. Most parents, however, feel relieved after a diagnosis has been made. Finally, they know why their child has been having difficulty.

"We were so relieved when the diagnosis was made," says Ben's mother. "At least there was a logical reason for why Ben was doing what he was doing."

TYPES OF MEDICATION

Attention deficit disorder cannot be cured with medication, but there are medications that temporarily help people with ADD to concentrate better and to control their behavior.

The type of medication prescribed for ADD depends on the individual. Some benefit from taking one kind of medication, while others benefit from taking another. People with only mild symptoms of ADD may not need medication at all. Behavior-management techniques used at home and at school may be sufficient to help these individuals manage their symptoms.

PEDIATRICIANS, NEUROLOGISTS, PSYCHIATRISTS, PSYCHOLOGISTS, AND SOCIAL WORKERS ARE ALL QUALIFIED TO EVALUATE A PERSON WHO MIGHT HAVE ADD.

Medication for treating the symptoms of ADD must be prescribed by a medical doctor. The doctor observes the patient's reaction to the medication and decides whether or not the patient is taking the proper type and amount. Adjustments often must be made after the person begins taking the medication, so it is important for the doctor to monitor the patient carefully.

About 75 percent of the people with ADD respond favorably to medication. Of the 25 percent who do not, most show only temporary improvement or no effect at all. A few become even more active, irritable, or agitated while they are taking medication. The only way for a doc-

A trained health professional can help young people with ADD and their parents to understand the nature of the condition and how to treat it effectively.

tor to know for certain how a person will react to a particular medication is to observe the patient's behavior over a period of time.

Stimulants

Stimulants are the most commonly prescribed medication for treating the symptoms of ADD. The three most frequently prescribed are Ritalin, Dexedrine, and Cylert. Of these, Ritalin is prescribed most often. While they are taking the medication, many individuals with ADD experience improvement in their ability to be organized, to focus attention, and to control their actions and emotions.

Ben's parents have seen improvement in Ben's behavior since he began taking medication. "The Ritalin seems to be helping Ben," says his mother. "He takes it twice a day, once in the morning and once at noontime."

Tricyclic Antidepressants and Clonidine

Tricyclic antidepressants are another class of medications found to be helpful in treating ADD. As their name implies, these drugs are also used to treat people with depression. These medications help to improve mood while reducing impulsiveness and frustration levels. The tricyclic antidepressant medications typically used in the treatment of the symptoms of ADD are Norpramin and Tofranil.

Clonidine has been used for many years to treat high blood pressure. It has also proven helpful in treating some individuals with ADD, especially those who are particularly aggressive or hot-tempered.

THE EFFECTS OF MEDICATION

Situation #1 described below illustrates the difficulty that a young person with ADD might have in completing a task. Situation #2 illustrates how medication might help make it easier for that person to complete the task.

Situation #1

Your best friend has asked you to make a list of all of the things you like about him or her. Seated at the desk in your room, you begin the list, but within a few seconds the phone rings and you have to answer it. When you go back to making the list, your little sister comes running through the room screaming. You look up to see what is going on and then go back to writing. Then your mother calls you to set the table for dinner. Shortly after you get back to your room, your mother calls you for dinner.

Your heart sinks as you realize that it will be impossible to finish the list because you still have all of your homework to do. You feel extremely frustrated. You know you have let your best friend down, and you worry that he or she will be angry or may not like you anymore.

In this situation, all the interruptions are caused by other people. For individuals with ADD, the brain causes the interruptions. It simply will not allow these individuals to concentrate on whatever task they are focusing on. The end result is the same, however. Although they want to complete the assignment, their work is left unfinished, and they feel frustrated.

Situation #2

Your best friend has asked you to make a list of all the things you like about him or her. You decide to go to the library after school to work on it. The library enforces a "quiet, please" rule and has study carrels to block out distractions. You have no trouble concentrating on your work. In ten minutes, you have completed the list and have enough time left to do all of your homework assignments before you have to be home for dinner. You walk home knowing that you have accomplished a great deal, and you feel proud. You are certain your best friend will be very pleased with the list you have made.

This situation illustrates how medication can make completing a task much easier for a person with ADD.

Working in a quiet environment that has few distractions, such as a study area of a library, can help a person with ADD focus on a task and successfully complete it.

The medication, like the library setting, helps people with ADD focus on their work without being distracted. They no longer feel so frustrated, and they can feel proud of their accomplishments and more confident about their ability to meet future obligations.

ADD IS NOT CURABLE, ALTHOUGH MUCH IS BEING DONE TO HELP YOUNG PEOPLE AND ADULTS WHO HAVE THE DISORDER TO BETTER MANAGE THEIR SYMPTOMS. THE MOST SUCCESSFUL TREATMENT INVOLVES A COMBINED USE OF MEDICATION, BEHAVIOR-MANAGEMENT TECHNIQUES, AND COUNSELING TO IMPROVE BEHAVIOR AND CONCENTRATION.

In cases in which treatment with medication is unsuccessful, other methods of treatment are available, such as the use of behavior-management techniques, counseling by an experienced professional, and instructional help in the classroom.

For individuals who respond favorably to medication, the most effective way to help them cope with their ADD symptoms is to combine the use of medication with the other methods of treatment.

BEHAVIOR MANAGEMENT

Medication can help people with ADD focus on a task and maintain control. A behavior-management program can help them change their behavior and feel more confident and hopeful as they approach daily tasks or assignments.

A professional, such as a psychologist, designs a behavior-management program tailored to the needs of the person with ADD. The techniques used in this program help the person improve his or her behavior and feel more successful in daily life. To keep track of progress, the professional who is overseeing the behavior-management program meets with this person in regularly scheduled counseling sessions, usually every week or every other week, depending on the individual's needs. Regular counseling sessions enable the therapist to modify the methods that are being used to help the person with ADD change his or her behavior. They also give the individual a chance to discuss any specific problems he or she is having. Periodically, the professional invites the person's entire family to the session. Meetings between the entire family and the therapist help keep the lines of communication open among family members, which makes their daily interactions easier and life happier for all.

The combined use of medication, counseling, and behavior-management techniques can improve the individual's relationships with family and friends. These methods can also help the student with ADD with his or her behavior and performance at school, especially if these methods are used along with special instructional help in the classroom. Changing behavior takes time, however, and setbacks are not unusual.

Behavior-Management Techniques
These behavior-management techniques have helped many young people with ADD work toward changing their behavior:

- *Charts* provide a record of progress as the person works on changing a behavior. This method can be used for young children and adolescents.

  The young person and his or her parents decide which daily behaviors need to improve: for example, completing homework, going to bed on time, or treating family members respectfully. They then agree upon an appropriate reward for success—extra time to watch television or to play computer games, for example.

The chart listing the days of the week and the behaviors to be changed is hung in a visible place in the house. A check mark is made on the chart on each day that the person has made the desired change in behavior. On every day that is checked off, the person earns a reward.

- *The token reward system* also works well for many young people in keeping track of changes in behavior.
  The young person and his or her parents choose one type of behavior they would like to improve. Together, they decide what type of tokens they will use—coins or plastic chips, for example. They then decide what special reward the tokens may be traded in for at the end of the week. The reward might be a toy or game, a food treat, or a special privilege. Each time the person demonstrates the desired behavior, he or she receives a token. At the end of the week, he or she trades in the tokens for the agreed-upon reward.

- *Making lists and writing notes* helps many young people remember tasks they might otherwise forget. Putting these lists and notes around the house as reminders helps them keep track of their responsibilities and chores. Sara, for instance, always keeps notes on her pillow because she knows she will use her pillow every day. Brian finds it helpful to tape notes onto his computer screen to remind him of school assignments and household chores.

- *Contracts* are often effective methods of managing behavior for teenagers. The teenager and his or her parents draw up a contract to be signed. Together, they decide what responsibility the teenager will assume and what the parents will provide if he or she meets this responsibility.

Sample Contract

I, _____ (name of teenager) agree to do the following:

_____

_____

_____

_____

If I am successful, I will receive the following privileges:

_____

_____

_____

_____

If I am not successful, I agree to accept the following consequences:

_____

_____

_____

_____

_____

Signature: _____

Date: _____

I, _____ (name of parent) agree to the terms described above. If _____ (name of teenager) lives up to his/her end of the agreement, I will grant the above privileges.

Signature:_____

Date:_____

For example, if a teenager is not coming home at a reasonable time on weekend nights, the contract might specify a time by which he or she must be home. The teenager agrees to be home by that time every weekend night for one month. In return, the parent might agree to drive the teenager to sports practice or music lessons every week. A parent might even agree to let an older teenager borrow the car once a week. If the teenager meets the terms of the contract, the parent must keep up his or her end of the bargain as well.

The next chapter discusses several methods available to help young people with ADD cope with their symptoms and meet the challenges presented to them at school.

MEETING CHALLENGES AT SCHOOL

The demands of school prove challenging, if not over-whelming, for most students with ADD. Research shows that three quarters of them fall one or more years behind in at least one subject. By adolescence, as many as one third of students with ADD have repeated at least one grade. Evan experienced difficulties from the time he entered preschool. Before a psychologist diagnosed him as having ADD, Evan had been expelled from two preschools for fighting with other children. He had to repeat first grade because he was so far behind his classmates in his work.

"I felt stupid because I got left back," explains Evan. "I was the only one in my class who wasn't promoted and I felt like a real dummy. I knew the other kids were making fun of me. And I also felt angry and ashamed because I couldn't control my temper. I didn't want to get into all those fights and always be sent to the principal's office, but it just happened."

Students like Evan do poorly not because they lack intelligence but because they have short attention spans, are easily distracted, and act impulsively. When students are unable to pay attention or to organize themselves, become easily distracted, and do not think before acting, it is harder for them to learn. In addition, much of what goes on in school, such as working math problems or writing spelling words, tends to be tedious, which makes it difficult for students with ADD to concentrate on these tasks.

School can be particularly problematic for hyperactive students. These young people have trouble staying seated and often blurt out answers before raising their hands or being called on by the teacher. They are likely to do their classroom assignments quickly and carelessly. Instead of working or paying attention in class, these students tend to be disruptive and may poke other students, slide out of their seats, or move around the room. It is also difficult for them to wait their turn in line, so they may push and shove.

Mark was hyperactive before being treated for ADD. He remembers what elementary school was like for him.

> *I just couldn't sit in my seat. I knew I had to finish my work, but no matter how hard I tried, I couldn't sit there and do it. All day long my teacher would say, "Sit down, Mark." Then the whole class would turn around and look at me. I felt so embarrassed. When my work wasn't finished, my teacher made me stay in at recess and finish it. Sometimes I still couldn't finish it. I would keep looking around the room or watching other kids walk down the hall. No matter how hard I tried, I couldn't do what was expected of me. And some of the kids in my class made fun of me. One girl always called me "Mark in the Dark" because she said I was so lost. I wanted to cry and punch her out all at the same time.*

Because they typically do not disrupt the class, students with ADD who are not hyperactive are less likely to come to the attention of the teacher. Therefore, it is often less obvious that the student has the disorder. Parents of these students may even receive praise from the teacher for their child's apparent good behavior. Nevertheless, school is likely to be a problem for these students, too. They tend to have trouble concentrating and may spend time daydreaming or staring out the window. They also tend to be easily distracted by what is going on around them and, as a result, may have just as much trouble completing their assignments as their hyperactive peers. These students may play with their pencils or make doodle drawings in their notebooks, for example, instead of doing their schoolwork.

Julie was not hyperactive; instead, she was quiet and withdrawn. "My problem was that I couldn't stop daydreaming," explains Julie. "The littlest thing would start me thinking of something else. Like if I was supposed to be doing a math paper, the plus sign would look like a cross and then I would start thinking about church. And then church would remind me of Sunday, and I would wonder if my grandparents were coming to visit on Sunday like they did sometimes. Then pretty soon, my teacher would be saying to turn in our papers and I would realize that I had only done two problems. But my teacher was really nice about it. She never made a big deal out of it. She always let me take my work home to finish it."

Julie also had trouble making friends. Because of her quiet and withdrawn personality, her classmates did not bother with her. The fact that she also suffered from an anxiety disorder caused her to feel especially self-conscious around other people, which only made matters worse.

When Julie was diagnosed with ADD, her teacher was surprised. "I never would have suspected that Julie had ADD," she says. "I was under the impression that students with ADD were disruptive in class. Julie was a model student in that respect. She was always quiet and always seemed to be trying so hard to do her work. I must admit, I was really off track. I knew Julie's parents had recently divorced and I just assumed that Julie was unable to complete her assignments because she was going through a difficult adjustment period. I guess that's why I always gave her extra time to complete her assignments. I had no idea that her difficulty stemmed from ADD."

DIFFICULTIES WITH SCHOOLWORK

There are many reasons why students with ADD tend to have problems with schoolwork, including the following:

Daydreaming. Students with ADD often find independent work difficult because their minds tend to wander. While reading or listening to their teachers, they are likely to lose track of where they are or what is being said. Because daydreaming interferes with concentration, these students may not learn material well.

• *Learning difficulties.* Some students with ADD also have learning difficulties, which make succeeding in school harder for them. One of these conditions is dyslexia, which involves problems with language communication. Students with dyslexia tend to have trouble reading, writing, and/or speaking.

Ben was diagnosed with dyslexia after he was diagnosed with ADD. He had difficulty with reading and often confused letters and words and had trouble recognizing words as he read. "Once I was diagnosed, the school assigned me a special reading teacher and a tutor to help me with reading every day," says Ben. "Eventually things got easier for me, but I still have trouble with reading. Sometimes my parents or friends have to read to me before I can understand my work. Sometimes they read into a tape recorder so that I can listen to the words over again if I need to."

• *Problems with organizational skills.* Many students with ADD have trouble with organizational skills, causing them to lose belongings such as books, pencils, and

61

notebooks. Often these students leave school without the books and papers they will need for homework that night. If they do their homework, they may forget to take it to school with them the next morning. Problems with organization also make it difficult to complete complex assignments, such as reports and term papers.

- *Problems with productivity.* Students with ADD tend to find it difficult to concentrate for long periods of time or to stick with a task, especially with tedious or repetitive assignments. As a result, they tend to fail to complete their work on time or at all.

- *Difficulty completing homework.* Trying to complete homework assignments can be very frustrating for students with ADD, which often leads to arguments between them and their parents, who constantly pressure them to finish their work. These students benefit from being allowed some time to relax after school before beginning their homework.

- *Poor handwriting.* For several reasons, many students with ADD have poor handwriting. Some students are impulsive, which causes them to be careless when forming letters and numbers. Others have difficulty writing because they think faster than their hands and fingers can move. Still others have trouble remembering letter formation, punctuation, capitalization, and grammar rules simultaneously. Poor handwriting is difficult for others to read and is also likely to hinder the student when studying notes taken in class or doing math computations. For example, a student who makes poorly formed numbers or who does not arrange the numbers in straight columns may make errors in computation.

- *Difficulty with changes.* Middle school and high school pose special challenges for students with ADD.

62

At these grade levels, students usually have several teachers, each one teaching a different subject in a different classroom. Students are expected to complete assignments with less assistance from teachers or parents. By the end of the school day, students with ADD may not remember what homework is due the next day or which books to take home. If they remember to do their homework, they may leave it at home or put it in their lockers in the morning and forget to hand it in during class.

- *Uneven performance.* Some students with ADD perform well in some subjects but poorly in others. Teachers and parents often believe that these students could do well in every subject if they tried harder. They often blame the students for being lazy or criticize them for not doing better. Steven, for instance, always did well in math. In other subjects, however, his performance was sometimes good and sometimes poor. Before being diagnosed with ADD, his parents and teachers accused him of being too lazy to try his best.

  "They would always say that if I would keep my mind on my work and stop fooling around, my other grades would be as good as my math grades," recalls Steven. "I wanted to concentrate and do well in all my subjects, but it was impossible for me. They didn't understand that I was trying really hard."

  After Steven was diagnosed with ADD, his parents and teachers became more understanding of his uneven school performance. With the help of medication, Steven found that he became better able to focus on his assignments, and his school performance improved as a result. Although math remained his strongest subject, his performance in other subjects improved as well.

- *Reaction to criticism.* When students perform poorly in school, the teacher may ask, "Why don't you ever

63

People with ADD often have poor handwriting, which makes it difficult for them to take notes in class and to do math computation.

finish your work?" or may say, "Use your brain and think." Failure in school and criticism from teachers, parents, or classmates often leave these students feeling frustrated and worthless. As a result, their school performance is likely to decline even more. School becomes increasingly difficult. Until students with ADD are diagnosed and treated, they usually experience a great deal of confusion and frustration. Although they try their best, nothing seems to turn out right. They may begin to think of themselves as stupid, and classmates may begin to think of them this way, also. For teenagers, rejection and failure may make them feel so disgusted that they want to drop out of school. That is what happened to Sara, who dropped out of high school in her junior year:

At school, I had a lot of trouble doing my school-work. I was always behind. Some of the kids made fun of me and called me "stupid" and "half brain" and things like that. I felt like a square peg trying to fit into a round hole. I hated school and I started to cut classes. I would just hang out in the bathroom. I got sent to the principal's office a lot, and I started to think I was bad. I didn't want to be a bad kid. I felt really down in the dumps about everything. I even thought I might be better off dead. Halfway through the school year, I dropped out.

In contrast, some students with ADD push themselves extra hard in an effort to succeed. Their parents may spend a great deal of time helping them with their schoolwork in an attempt to keep them from failing. Julie's mother worked with Julie every afternoon after school. The only way Julie was able to complete her assignments and not fall behind was with her mother's help. Although this approach usually works for a while, these students tend to become frustrated eventually. Fortunately, there are strategies that can help young people with ADD succeed in school.

STRATEGIES FOR SUCCESS IN THE CLASSROOM

Although young people with ADD are entitled by law to special school services, such as special-education classes, most students with ADD are able to learn and succeed in a regular classroom if they are given extra help and attention. Various techniques may be used to increase the learning potential of these students.

- *Parental involvement.* Parents can help children succeed in school by discussing the student's strengths and weaknesses with teachers even before the school year begins. It is important for teachers and parents to work together as a team. The teachers' efforts at school should be supported by the parents at home, and communication between teachers and parents should be open and frequent.

- *Patient and caring teachers.* Students with ADD benefit most from teachers who are patient and warm and who give them as much encouragement and praise as possible.

- *Structure in the classroom.* The ideal classroom environment for students with ADD is one that has a great deal of structure and organization. These students tend to perform best when teachers make rules and regulations clear and when they keep the schedule of activities predictable and regular.

- *Special seating.* Students with ADD seem to have greater success in school when they sit away from windows and doorways, where they are less likely to be distracted by outside activities. Some students find that working at a study carrel helps them to concentrate.

- *Simplified instructions.* The more simple and clear that teachers make instructions, the better it is for students with ADD. By giving one instruction at a time instead of a series of instructions, teachers can help these students to follow procedures and complete tasks. Students also may benefit from having a classmate repeat the teacher's instructions to be sure they have heard them correctly.

• *Shortened assignments.* Many students with ADD find it difficult to stick with repetitive tasks or to concentrate on one subject for a long period of time. To help them, the teacher may break down assignments into smaller components. Instead of asking these students to do every math problem on a page, for instance, the teacher might ask them to do every other one.

• *Simplified assignments.* Students with ADD tend to have problems with complex assignments, such as reports and term papers, because they have trouble with organization. Parents or teachers can help them by breaking down complex projects into smaller, more manageable segments. Students can then work to complete each task, one at a time, until the whole project is completed.

TEACHERS AND PARENTS CAN HELP STUDENTS WITH ADD BY:

STRUCTURING THE ENVIRONMENT

PROVIDING PATIENCE AND SUPPORT

SIMPLIFYING INSTRUCTIONS

ALLOWING EXTRA TIME TO COMPLETE ASSIGN-MENTS

HELPING WITH REPORTS AND TERM PAPERS

BREAKING LARGE TASKS INTO SMALLER, MORE MANAGEABLE ONES

• *Extra time.* Students with ADD benefit from having extra time to complete classroom assignments and tests. Some teachers even give students with ADD oral tests, which avoids problems with handwriting and concentration.

- *Word processors and tape recorders.* Word processors can be of great help to students with ADD who have difficulty writing by hand. If a word processor is not available, these students may be able to dictate to their parents, who can write down the assignment for them. For longer assignments, some students with ADD find it easier to record the material for their report on a tape recorder and present it to the teacher or the class in this way.

- *Help with organization.* Because of the problems they have in organizing themselves and their belongings, many students with ADD benefit from help from teachers, parents, and even other students in keeping their books, notebooks, and desks in order. Problems with organization cause many students with ADD to go home at the end of the day without all of the materials they will need for homework that night. These students benefit from having two sets of books, one for school and one for home, to avoid the problem of leaving books behind.

- *Photocopied and highlighted textbooks.* It is often helpful for the teacher to photocopy a chapter from a textbook and then highlight the most important parts for students with ADD. This decreases the amount of material these students must read and comprehend, which helps to lessen the amount of time they must spend reading and studying.

- *Concentration tapes.* Many students find that listening to audiotapes that beep every thirty to sixty seconds helps them to concentrate and stay on task. The beep reminds them to refocus on the assignment rather than

Word processors can be helpful tools for students
with ADD who have difficulty writing by hand.

daydream or doodle. These tapes can be used at school for classroom assignments and at home for homework assignments.

• *Assignment pads.* Many students with ADD find it useful to keep an assignment pad in which they write down homework assignments and other tasks at the end of each school day. As an additional help, the teacher might initial the bottom of the page to confirm that all the assigned work has been written down. At home, the student's parents can read the assignment page and then initial it to acknowledge that they are aware of what work the student had to complete.

• *Charts.* Charts have helped many students with ADD to improve their behavior and performance at school. The teacher evaluates a student's behavior and performance each day. A number, or score, is given for each subject every school day. The student takes the chart home to his or her parents at the end of the day. Good performance is rewarded, such as with a special dessert or permission to stay up an extra hour that night. On unsuccessful days, there is no reward.

The progress of high school students can be charted weekly rather than daily. Charts can be used to track students' grades on tests and term papers. Teachers can also list upcoming quizzes and projects at the bottom of the charts so that the students' parents can help plan study time and organize study material.

• *Nontraditional environments.* Some high school students have trouble following a traditional academic curriculum. Work-study programs and vocational-technical schools are positive options for them. In a work-study program, students attend school for half the day and work at a job the other half. This program helps to vary their days and reduce the monotony many of them feel within a traditional academic environment. Vocational-technical schools teach trades, such as auto mechanics and offer a more hands-on approach to learning, which can be beneficial to students with ADD.

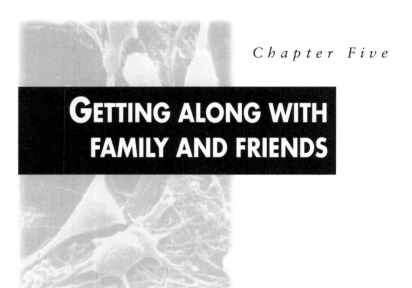

Chapter Five

GETTING ALONG WITH FAMILY AND FRIENDS

Attention deficit disorder affects not only the individuals who have it, but also their parents, siblings, classmates, teammates, and friends.

RELATIONSHIPS WITH PARENTS

All parents want their children to behave well, to succeed in school, and to have many friends. A child with ADD may have difficulty achieving these goals, however. It is likely that the parents of a child diagnosed with ADD have lived through many years of frustration, struggling to understand their child's hyperactive, impulsive, and inattentive behavior. Parents also experience many conflicting emotions when they learn that their child has a lifelong chronic condition.

Young people with ADD tend to have difficulty following rules because they are inattentive and impulsive. For example, an individual with ADD may start to clean his or her room when told to, but then part way through the task will start doing something else. If told to stop climbing on the furniture, a child with ADD is likely to stop for a while and then impulsively start again.

As a result, parents of these young people often feel frustrated or on edge. They may believe that the behavior problems are somehow their fault, that if they were better parents, their children would be better behaved. Other people will also sometimes accuse them of not being good enough or strict enough parents, which only compounds their feelings of frustration and depression.

In turn, young people with ADD may also feel angry, sad, or frustrated over their relationships with their parents. They do not understand why they receive so much criticism and punishment. They are likely to feel sad that their parents are upset and unhappy with them, and they strive to behave well and win their parents' approval. "I felt horrible about the way I acted," says Brian. "I didn't have any friends because of my behavior. The other kids never asked me to play and I never got invited to parties. I felt really bad about it. I wanted them to like me.

"One night after I went to bed, I overheard my mom and dad talking and my mom was crying. I heard her tell my dad that she felt sad because I acted the way I did and because I didn't have any friends. I felt awful. I knew I was a real disappointment to her. I thought about running away."

When a parent of a child with ADD also has the disorder, the family problems are even more complicated. Fortunately, however, once a diagnosis is made, life at home usually begins to improve. When parents learn what ADD is and what can be done to cope with its symptoms, they are likely to feel relieved and hopeful. "After Brian was diagnosed," says Brian's mother, "I realized that I had many of the same symptoms. Eventually, I, too, was diagnosed with ADD, and medication was prescribed. The medication has made a big difference. Now I feel I can relate to Brian better because of my own coping with ADD."

Behavior-Management Techniques at Home

Many parents find that using behavior-management techniques helps to alleviate tension and conflict between them and their children. For example, parents can help their son or daughter to complete chores by being specific about what is expected. If the young person's job is to set the table for dinner, for instance, the parent can write step-by-step instructions on an index card. For example:

1. Get plates and glasses from cabinet.
2. Get forks, knives, and spoons from drawer.
3. Fold napkins.
4. Set places at table.

Because young people with ADD often get sidetracked from what they are doing and because it is hard for them to plan ahead, referring to simply written instructions like this may help. If they forget what they are supposed to do, they can look at the card as a reminder. This method can also be used for homework assignments. To reinforce success, parents can reward the young person with a hug or words of praise whenever the chore or assignment is completed properly. If it is an especially difficult chore or an important school project that the young person accomplishes, a special reward may be appropriate.

RELATIONSHIPS WITH BROTHERS AND SISTERS

Siblings have uniquely close, intimate relationships that form some of the strongest, most enduring bonds in a person's life. Brothers and sisters help to shape one another's lives and prepare each other for experiences they will have with peers and as adults.

Siblings of young people with ADD often find home life as difficult as their parents do. They may feel angry, guilty, or even afraid. Before they understand what ADD is, they may feel angry that their brother or sister causes so much commotion around the house. Some may wonder if it is their fault that their brother or sister has ADD. Others may wonder if ADD is contagious.

Age plays a part in how a sibling relates to the affected brother or sister who has ADD. Older siblings may tend to avoid their brother or sister. Because they are upset or frustrated with his or her behavior, they may spend as little time as possible with this sibling. In public, older siblings often feel embarrassed by the inappropriate behavior of a brother or sister with ADD.

"Every time we went somewhere, my brother, Evan, embarrassed me," says Chad. "In the store, he would throw a fit if my mom wouldn't buy him what he wanted. Sometimes, he would even hit my mom. She never knew what to do. People were always looking at us. It was horrible. I just wanted to evaporate."

For younger siblings, the situation is a little different. They, too, will often try to avoid being around their brother or sister with ADD, but usually not because they are embarrassed. Instead, they are often afraid. Chad and Evan's little sister, Michelle, hid under her bed whenever Evan acted up. "I knew I would be safe under my bed," says Michelle. "Evan was too big to fit under my little bed and I knew he couldn't hit me if I stayed under there."

Feelings of Resentment

The extra attention that young people with ADD receive from their parents sometimes makes their siblings feel left out and neglected. If you have a sibling, you may remember times when you felt that your parents gave your sibling more attention than they gave you. You may have felt envious or resentful. These feelings are normal. Siblings of a young person with ADD often feel this way even when the attention is given in the form of punishment or criticism.

Attention deficit disorder can affect a person's relationships with parents, siblings, and friends. Honest communication and understanding are the key to strengthening those relationships.

Often, once they learn about ADD, siblings have a better understanding of why their brother or sister acts a certain way, and they try to help. Allison remembers her experiences with her sister, Beth:

I hated my sister, Beth, for all the time my mom and dad had to spend on her, mostly yelling at her. She would never do what she was supposed to do. Her clothes were all over the floor, not just in her room, but all over the house. Whenever she was supposed to do something, it never got done. Mom and Dad would yell, and then they would make me go and do what Beth was supposed to. That wasn't fair.

After my parents took Beth to the doctor and found out that Beth had ADD, they explained all about it to me, including why Beth acted the way she did. I really felt sorry for her because I knew she couldn't help it. Now I try not to get mad at her and I try to help her with her chores.

Sometimes, the young person with ADD resents his or her siblings. This tends to happen when parents blame the son or daughter with ADD for everything that goes wrong within the sibling relationship. Parents often automatically assume that the child with ADD instigated the tension or argument. This leads that individual to feel angry and resentful toward the siblings. Jeremy resented his sister, Jessica, because she frequently got him into trouble.

My sister, Jessica, teased me a lot. She said things that made me mad, and she would go into my room and snoop through my stuff. She knew I didn't want her in my room. Then if I called her a name or slapped her, she would run to my parents. Jessica would only tell them the part of the story about the things I did to her, never what she had done to me. I would try to say my part, but my parents would believe her. I would get in trouble. Then I would feel like crying or throwing something because it just wasn't fair. They always took her side and I was always the bad one, no matter what. I ended up hating Jessica. We're doing okay now, though.

Building Bridges of Communication

The most important thing parents can do to help their children get along is to open the lines of communication among all members of the family and to make certain that everyone understands the nature of ADD.

Here are some other ways to develop more positive relationships among siblings:

- *Appreciate each individual's needs.* The needs of the children without ADD often take second place to the ongoing needs of the young person with ADD. Parents should make a special effort to spend time with each of their children, preferably one at a time.

- *Involve siblings in the treatment process.* After a young person is diagnosed with ADD, it is often beneficial for his or her siblings to become part of the treatment process. If there are major problems within the family, the therapist sometimes will suggest certain behavior-management techniques to be used with all of the siblings, not just the one with ADD. The rewards for improved behavior might then be family rewards, such as a family trip to the amusement park, the beach, or the movies.

Holly and her sisters, Becky and Cindy, argued constantly. Holly found it difficult to listen to others and to think ahead. She would often borrow clothes and other items from her sisters without first asking their permission. She would then forget to return the items. When her sisters would ask her about their things, Holly would claim not to know where they were. This was true; she could not find them in the disorganized mess in her room. An argument would start immediately, and before long, the girls would be screaming and hitting each other. Holly was also often excluded from things Becky and Cindy did together. This hurt Holly's feelings and made her feel angry. She would call her sisters names, which would trigger another argument.

After Holly was diagnosed with ADD at the age of fourteen, the therapist suggested that the family keep a chart. Each day that passed without an argument, the girls could put a check mark on the chart. If they were able to make it through an entire week without fighting, they would be allowed to choose a family treat.

"It took us a few weeks before we reached our goal," says Holly. "At first it was really hard to get through a day without fighting. I didn't think we would ever make it through a week. When we did, we were all surprised. We love Chinese food, so we all went to a Chinese restaurant for dinner as our reward. I try to think ahead more, and my sisters try to be more patient with me. We don't fight nearly as much anymore."

RELATIONSHIPS WITH PEERS

Relationships with friends are important to all young people. Forming relationships with people of the same age helps young people, especially teenagers, define their personalities and develop self-confidence.

Because of their often disruptive or disorganized behavior, young people with ADD tend to have trouble making and keeping friends. At school, their classmates may reject them because they cannot wait their turn or because they blurt out answers in class. At recess, their classmates may be turned off by their aggressive behavior. Neighborhood children may refuse to play with them because of their bossiness and their insistence on creating and enforcing all of the rules. Unfortunately, young people with ADD are likely to find themselves with no friends at all, or with only younger friends, who are more apt to put up with their behavior.

For teenagers, who are beginning to assert their independence from their parents, the desire for peer companionship is especially strong. As a result, teenagers with ADD sometimes do things that they think will win them acceptance by the "in crowd." They may brag, lie, or steal, for example. Some may use drugs or alcohol. Unfortunately, this behavior is likely to add to the problems these teens already have.

Problems with Teammates

Young people with ADD often have difficulty in team sports or in group games. The problem may be that they behave aggressively or cannot keep their attention on the game. It may even be because they are clumsy; people with ADD often have poor coordination. Mark recalls his experiences on the ball field:

> *When I was in elementary school, I wanted to play on the softball team. I had a problem from the first day. The coach put me in the outfield. That was a mistake. There weren't too many balls that came out where I was standing, so pretty soon, I was looking around and watching other things that were going on around me. I remember there was a man walking his dog and the dog kept chasing its tail. I thought that was funny. Then I watched a group of kids ride their bikes over a hill they had made out of dirt. They would ride fast up one side of the hill and then come crashing down on the other side.*
>
> *When the ball finally came my way, I wasn't paying any attention. It rolled right past me. This kid on third base called me "cotton brain" and I*

With proper treatment of the symptoms of ADD, a
person may find it easier to get along with friends
and participate in group activities.

got really mad. I ran over to him and started to wrestle with him. The coach made us sit on the bench for the rest of practice. I felt angry that I couldn't play.

I ended up getting totally thrown off the team a few weeks later and I felt really bad about that. I knew I wasn't doing what I was supposed to, but I couldn't help it. My mom ended up signing me up for karate lessons instead, and I did okay with that, but I really wanted to play baseball. Since my ADD was diagnosed two years ago, and I started taking Ritalin and working on controlling my behavior, I've been able to join the baseball team. I don't play outfield anymore because I get too distracted out there. My coach says I'm an excellent player, and he told me I'll have no trouble playing on the high school team next year.

THE BENEFITS OF TREATMENT

Treatment of the symptoms of ADD with the use of medication, behavior-management techniques, and counseling can help young people to overcome many of their social difficulties. Once their behavior improves, these individuals tend to become more fun to be around. As a result, they usually find it easier to establish solid, long-lasting friendships. After treatment, even teenagers who have gotten involved with the wrong crowd tend to be more able to find new, more appropriate friends.

Sara became involved with the wrong crowd after she dropped out of school. She and her friends experimented with alcohol and drugs and even admitted to shoplifting on a few occasions. Fortunately, Sara's mother was able to convince her daughter to see a psychiatrist, who diagnosed Sara with ADD and treated her symptoms with the drug Cylert and with regular counseling. "I'm working on making new friends now," says Sara. "The medication and the counseling sessions with my doctor have helped me a lot. I feel like I'm finally getting back on track."

THE PROBLEMS A YOUNG PERSON WITH ADD HAS BECAUSE OF HYPERACTIVITY, IMPULSIVE-NESS, OR INATTENTION OFTEN ADD MUCH TEN-SION TO FAMILY LIFE. FORTUNATELY, ONCE A DIAGNOSIS IS MADE AND THE FAMILY LEARNS WHAT ADD IS AND WHAT CAN BE DONE TO HELP SOMEONE WITH THE DISORDER, FAMILY LIFE USU-ALLY BECOMES SMOOTHER AND HAPPIER FOR EVERYONE.

For some young people with ADD, treatment of the symptoms is not enough to help them make and keep friends. They must also be taught how to relate better to their peers. Parents can help by guiding their sons or daughters in choosing friends and in coping with peer rejection. Parents also can help develop their children's social skills by role-playing with their children or by taking them to group-therapy sessions in which the skills are taught.

Julie recalls that her mother helped her to develop friendships with some of her classmates. "My mom encouraged me to invite one or two girls from school to go to the movies and to go roller skating. We had a great time and found out that we enjoyed being together. Now that I'm in high school, I'm thinking of joining some clubs in order to make more friends. I realize that I'm able to be a good friend to other people and that I'm likable."

In the next chapter, the young people in this book tell how they are successfully coping with their condition in their everyday lives, and they reveal their dreams for the future. Barbara and Robert, two adults who coped with the symptoms of ADD throughout childhood and adolescence before being diagnosed, also tell their stories.

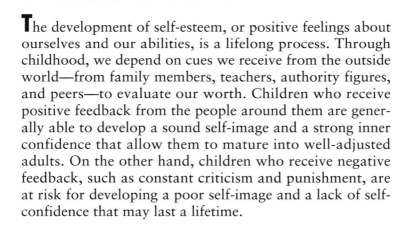

THE POWER OF SELF-ESTEEM

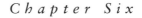

The development of self-esteem, or positive feelings about ourselves and our abilities, is a lifelong process. Through childhood, we depend on cues we receive from the outside world—from family members, teachers, authority figures, and peers—to evaluate our worth. Children who receive positive feedback from the people around them are generally able to develop a sound self-image and a strong inner confidence that allow them to mature into well-adjusted adults. On the other hand, children who receive negative feedback, such as constant criticism and punishment, are at risk for developing a poor self-image and a lack of self-confidence that may last a lifetime.

THE EFFECTS OF ADD ON SELF-ESTEEM

Young people with ADD often have low self-esteem because of their long history of personal frustrations and difficult relationships. As infants, many were so sensitive to touch and so restless and irritable that they cried when their parents held them. As they got older, these children faced difficulties at school. They often experienced failure and rejection, which made them feel that they were not as good as other children. At home, they were so often punished for inappropriate behavior that they began to think of themselves as bad people.

By the time these young people reach middle school or high school, they often feel that they do not fit in with their peers, that they will never be accepted by others, and that they will never live up to their own or other people's expectations. Many also feel embarrassed and frustrated by their impulsiveness, which causes them to lose their tempers easily, adding to their social problems. Brian recalls his experiences with classmates:

> *I was always in trouble. The kids at school teased me because I got mad so easily. They liked to see me angry. The more they teased me, the angrier I got, and I would usually end up in a fist fight. Then my teacher would send me to the principal's office or give me detention. I knew nobody liked me, so after awhile I didn't care how I acted. I started acting worse and worse in school and ended up getting suspended a lot. I didn't care because I hated it there anyway. I hated myself, too. I knew I was different.*

All young people want to succeed. They want to be accepted and respected, and they want to win the approval of others. When young people with ADD do not meet their own expectations or those of parents, teachers, and peers, their self-esteem is likely to suffer. Fortunately, there are ways for these young people to learn to feel good about themselves.

DEVELOPING A POSITIVE SELF-IMAGE

Every time you succeed in learning a new skill, your sense of self-esteem increases. Think about the first time you

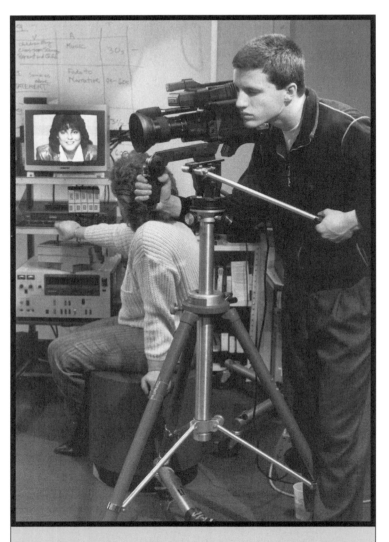

Vocational-technical schools and workshops can be positive environments for students with ADD, who may need diverse tasks to keep from being bored, or may prefer a hands-on approach to learning.

were able to read a book or ride a bicycle without help. You probably felt proud of your accomplishment. These good feelings about your achievements help you to develop a positive self-image. Many young people with ADD have learned to develop positive feelings about themselves through their accomplishments.

Here are some strategies for building self-esteem:

- *Focus on strengths.* One way for young people with ADD to develop a positive self-image is to focus on activities that they enjoy doing. Being good at something or knowing a lot about a subject can help these young people feel good about themselves. A person who loves to draw and paint, for instance, might take an art class after school. Those who are interested in airplanes might build models from kits or visit an airport and talk with airline personnel.

  Young people who enjoy sports might join a community or school soccer, basketball, or softball team. Those who do not do well in team sports might try a class in karate, tennis, swimming, or dance. Parents can help their sons or daughters practice the skills needed to participate in these activities and can attend games and performances to show support for their children's efforts.

WHEN YOUNG PEOPLE WITH ADD DO NOT MEET THEIR OWN EXPECTATIONS OR THOSE OF PARENTS, TEACHERS, AND PEERS, THEIR SELF-ESTEEM IS LIKELY TO SUFFER.

- *Set reasonable goals.* It is often difficult for young people with ADD to meet responsibilities. Parents and teachers can help by defining a task that can be completed successfully. The goal must be one that the young person is likely to achieve. This might be a special job, such as watering the household plants, taking out the trash, setting the table for dinner, or helping with repair projects around the house. When the person achieves the goal, he or she should be praised for a job well done. Beth, who is now thirteen, explains an experience that helped her feel more confident and positive about herself:

I love cats. A friend's cat had kittens and I wanted to keep one of them. My parents said that I could if I took care of it myself. I was worried that I wouldn't do a good job because I always had so much trouble following through on chores around the house. My sister, Allison, helped me make a chart that had a schedule for feeding the kitten and cleaning its litter box. The chart listed all of the days of the week, and I could check off each day that I fed the cat and changed the litter.

Butterscotch is a year old now and she's very healthy. My parents and sister say they're proud of the way I take care of her. The veterinarian told me I'm doing a good job, too, and that really made me feel good. I want to work with animals when I'm older.

- *Strive for achievement.* Taking a job after school and working a few hours a week can help create a sense of accomplishment while at the same time provide a paycheck. Volunteer work is another gratifying option for teenagers; hospitals and nursing homes always welcome extra help. Many teens also find that they enjoy working with their hands, so building models, working with wood or clay, and cooking and baking, for example, can be positive experiences for them. Jeremy, a high school senior, discovered that he had a knack for horticulture.

I wasn't really good at anything. I wasn't in the band and I didn't play sports. I wasn't a good student, either. I used to envy kids who were good at things. I always wished I could be like them. A couple of years ago, things changed. I went with a friend and his parents to a plant show at the mall, and there was a small section on orchids. The man who worked there said that orchids were very hard to grow and there was a certain knack to it. He said that most people had no luck.

After I got home, I kept thinking about the orchids and what the man had said and I decided that I wanted to try to grow one. I asked my mom if she could drive me back to the mall and loan me some money to buy one. She was so happy that I was finally interested in something that she agreed even though the whole project was pretty expensive. I did some chores around the house and I mowed the lawn for a few of our neighbors to earn the money.

I found that I liked the challenge of taking care of the orchid and seeing if I could keep it alive. Well, I still have it and it's doing great. I also got much more involved in plants and I have most of the basement set up with grow lights and all sorts of plants. My dad put a small greenhouse on the back of our house so that the plants could mature. Last spring, I even sold some of them right in front of our house. I got a lot of compliments on how healthy and colorful my plants were. I'm working part-time at a nursery now so that I can learn how to run one because I'm hoping to have a nursery of my own someday.

- *Expect and accept setbacks.* The road to success is usually not a smooth one; there will almost always be pitfalls and detours along the way. It is more constructive for young people with ADD to look at setbacks, such as turning in a report late or not finishing a chore, as opportunities to try again and to continue to learn and grow rather than as failures.

SUCCESS STORIES

The young people you met in this book were courageous and open enough to share their stories with you. All of them—as well as Barbara and Robert, the two adults you will meet—have found ways to live with the symptoms of ADD, build their confidence and self-esteem, and improve the quality of their lives. They have done this in unique ways, suited to their individual abilities, personalities, and lifestyles.

Brian
Brian recently entered a writing contest held at his school and won first prize. He then entered a statewide writing competition and won second prize. He has taken the first step in realizing his dream of becoming a famous writer and film producer. "I feel like I can really do it," says Brian. "Winning this award convinced me that I really do have talent."

Michael
Michael, who is now twelve years old, is still hyperactive, although medication is helping him. His parents and teachers still use behavior-management techniques, such as charting and token rewards, to help him control his behavior. "I don't mind having ADD," Michael says. "That's just the way I am, and it really doesn't bother me. I think I'm smart and likable." Michael thinks his extra energy helps him to excel in sports. He enjoys soccer, softball, and karate. He hopes to become a sportscaster someday.

Evan

With the help of Ritalin and the use of behavior-management techniques, ten-year-old Evan has made progress. "I'm much happier with myself now," says Evan. "I don't have as many temper outbursts as I used to and I feel good about that. Other kids seem to like me more now, too."

Since Evan's diagnosis with ADD, Evan, Chad, Michelle, and their parents have become a happier, more relaxed family. Their mother especially feels their success:

> *We have grown much closer as a result of Evan's diagnosis. We have learned so much about ourselves and others. Evan's ADD has given me the courage and determination to go back to school and pursue a career in teaching. Looking back at my childhood, I feel that I had many of the same problems Evan has had. Although I was never diagnosed with ADD, I feel that my problems in school were probably related to it. I grew up thinking I was stupid. No one told me otherwise. For Evan, things are different. There is so much more knowledge about ADD today. Evan is truly brilliant and creative, and he has a strong desire to learn and to succeed. His father and I are making sure he knows that he is a smart, important person.*

MANY YOUNG PEOPLE WITH ADD HAVE LEARNED TO DEVELOP POSITIVE FEELINGS ABOUT THEMSELVES THROUGH THEIR ACCOMPLISHMENTS.

In his free time, Evan enjoys collecting foreign coins and swimming. "But I especially like reading about prehistoric times," says Evan. "A few weeks ago my parents took me to a museum where I got to see dinosaur skeletons and an exhibit of mechanical dinosaurs that moved. The room was set up to look the way the earth looked in the days when dinosaurs lived. It was awesome! I love science and I want to be a paleontologist."

Steven

Steven's school performance improved as a result of treatment with medication and the use of behavior-management techniques. Although Steven had always done well in math, the treatment of his ADD symptoms enabled him to become a good all-around student. Today he is eighteen and a high school senior. He has been accepted to college on a football scholarship.

I got a lot of criticism before I was diagnosed with ADD. My teachers criticized me for not doing my work and for not doing it right, and my parents criticized me for not finishing chores around the house. All the criticism made me feel like a failure. Once I got help, things turned around for me. Being accepted to college and winning the scholarship has made me feel really good about myself. I feel proud of what I've accomplished. I still dream of playing on a professional football team, and I believe I will.

Sara

"I'm back in school and doing pretty well," says Sara, who is now in eleventh grade. "I've changed a lot. I'm getting good grades now, and the kids at school seem to like the new me. At home, I'm getting along better with my mom. We still argue sometimes, but my therapist has helped us learn ways of dealing with our problems and with each other. We use contracts, and things are working out much better now."

Art is Sara's favorite subject in school. She especially enjoys making pottery and sculpting with clay. She plans to go to art school after finishing high school.

Julie

Julie is now fifteen and in her first year of high school. She seems to have control over both her ADD symptoms and her anxiety-disorder symptoms.

"Julie still needs much reassurance," says her mother, "but she has no trouble sharing her feelings with me. I try to be honest and I try to keep communication open. I encourage independence in Julie and I try to give her as many opportunities to succeed as possible. She is growing into a fine young lady and I am very proud of her."

"I joined the chorus at my school and I've made a few friends," says Julie. "I would like to be a music teacher someday."

Ben

The combined use of Ritalin and behavior-management techniques has been helping thirteen-year-old Ben control his hyperactive and impulsive behaviors and has enabled him to become a better student. Although he still wrestles with reading because of his dyslexia, he has made great strides in school.

Ben loves animals and spends every summer on his grandfather's farm, where his grandfather gives him the opportunity to feed and care for the animals. "The most amazing thing was when I got to see a foal actually being born," Ben says. "It was really incredible. The best part was that my grandfather said I could have the foal for my own. She's full grown now and she's beautiful. I'm hoping to run my grandfather's farm myself when I'm older."

"Ben has an interesting way of looking at things," says Ben's grandfather. "He approaches life with enthusiasm and a sense of humor, and he has an ability to see more detail in things than most people. Ben believes this is a result of having ADD."

Mark

Fourteen-year-old Mark is doing well in school and is looking forward to beginning high school next year. "When I do well in school and get along with my friends, my whole life seems to be better," says Mark. "I feel a lot better about myself, too." This past year, Mark made the honor roll and joined the baseball team. One of his favorite hobbies is building models, and he thinks he might like to become an architect someday.

Holly

At sixteen, Holly is now in high school. Regular counseling and a behavior-management program have helped Holly succeed in taking on and meeting new and exciting challenges. She has joined the photography club and has discovered that she is a talented photographer. She has entered photography contests at her school and in her community, and she has received awards.

Before Holly began treatment for her ADD symptoms, her problem with inattention always made it difficult for her to make and keep friends. "I hated myself," she says. "I was very unpopular at school, and at home my sisters argued with me all the time. I knew nobody liked me. I used to dream about how great it would be to go away and then come back as someone else. I wanted to be someone that everyone liked.

"Now, finally, I'm being noticed for something good," says Holly. "I get a lot of compliments about my photographs from my classmates and that makes me feel good. I don't have to walk through the halls feeling like everyone is talking about how weird I am. After school, I volunteer at the hospital and I've met a lot of nice people. I feel good about being able to help them. I'm much happier with myself now."

Holly hopes to have a career in social work.

To build self-esteem, people with ADD should focus on the special skills they have and the activities they enjoy.

TWO ADULTS WITH ADD

Barbara and Robert were not diagnosed with ADD until they reached adulthood. The road to adulthood was bumpy for them, but they found ways to cope with their symptoms all through childhood, adolescence, and young adulthood. Both went on to create successful lives and are doing even better now that they are receiving help in coping with their ADD symptoms.

Both Barbara and Robert feel relieved that a diagnosis has finally been made. They understand themselves better now that they have learned about the disorder. Barbara and Robert are optimistic about managing their ADD symptoms, and their accomplishments have helped both of them develop positive self-images.

Barbara's Story

Barbara is twenty-six years old and was diagnosed with ADD last year. She remembers her childhood as one filled with problems both at home and at school. She had trouble getting along with her family because her brother criticized her for being absent-minded and for losing things, and her parents criticized her for being lazy and irresponsible. At school, she had trouble concentrating because she frequently daydreamed, which meant she rarely finished an assignment on time or heard instructions the first time they were given to her.

When Barbara was in high school, she began to feel depressed much of the time. She felt that her future would be gloomy. She relied on alcohol to help her to feel better, and even tried drugs a few times. The turning point came the summer after her junior year in high school when her family went to the beach on vacation. During the vacation, Barbara made some friends who taught her how to sail and water ski.

"I found that I had a gift for these sports," Barbara says. "I had never been successful at anything before. It felt wonderful to finally be good at something."

The following summer, Barbara was able to get a job at the beach and take sailing lessons. At the end of the summer, the owner of the sailing school offered her a permanent job as an assistant. She worked there for a few years and improved her sailing skills so much that she is now a professional crew member on sailboats that race all over the world.

Despite her success with sailing, Barbara's problems with being forgetful and losing things continued. She frequently misplaced things, and her apartment was always a mess. She never felt organized. Barbara wanted to understand why she had these problems, and she sought help from a psychiatrist.

The psychiatrist evaluated Barbara and determined that she had ADD. He prescribed medication, but it did not have an effect on her, so it was discontinued. To help Barbara with her symptoms, the psychiatrist meets with her regularly and uses behavior-management techniques. Barbara feels that she has made progress. She is proud of her accomplishments and feels that having ADD has actually helped her in life.

"Having ADD has its bright spots," Barbara says. "I feel much enthusiasm for the goals I try to meet. I have a lot of determination and I know how to rely on myself. I am very independent and I like that."

Robert's Story

Robert , age forty, is a chiropractor with a successful practice. He was thirty-seven when a doctor diagnosed him with ADD.

I knew all my life that I had a problem, but I just didn't know what it was. I thought I was fairly intelligent, but my teachers would always criticize me for not working up to my potential. My grades were mostly C's. My teachers said I could do better if I tried harder. I wasn't able to work any harder, though. I was so easily distracted. I couldn't concentrate for more than a little while. And I was a great procrastinator. I always put off doing things until later. I always had piles of papers and books and things lying around.

Another problem I had was not looking ahead. I did what I felt like doing at that moment without any thought about the future. If I was supposed to be doing my homework, but a book on my bookshelf caught my eye, I would immediately drop the homework and begin reading the book. I would forget all about the homework until the next day at school when the teacher would ask for it to be handed in.

My mind was always racing, and I was sharply aware of everything that was going on around me. I would notice the ticking of the clock at the same time that a bird flying by the window would capture my attention at the same time I would be studying the design of the wallpaper. While all this was going on, I would be thinking about stock car racing, which I love. I called myself mentally hyper. I was also physically hyperactive. My fingers were always tapping and my legs were always jumping.

I found it easy to make friends because I love to talk. But it was the talking that got me into trouble. I always monopolized conversations and people were turned off by this. When the other person would begin to speak, my mind would immediately wander and I would tune him or her out. Since I wasn't a good listener, the other person would soon become insulted and would no longer want to associate with me.

My intelligence got me through college and I went on to have a successful chiropractic practice. My occupation has proven to be perfect for me because I like a lot of variety in my life. I'm easily bored. In my practice, I see a patient for fifteen or twenty minutes and then I'm on to the next patient. This keeps me interested and helps me keep my mind on what I'm doing.

I'm taking Ritalin now and feel that it's helping me to be more focused and less impulsive. It helps me to look ahead and plan. I still procrastinate, but not nearly so much as before. I'm also in a support group now, and I've learned through other adults with ADD that both exercise and meditation can help with learning how to focus and concentrate. I've also learned that if I stand closer to people with whom I'm speaking and establish more eye contact, I'm able to be more attentive to what they're saying. I'm able to develop better relationships with people now, which makes me feel good.

RESOURCES

Each of these organizations is willing to share information about the nature of its work and its special focus on ADD.

Children with Attention Deficit Disorder (CHADD)
499 NW 70th Avenue, Suite 308
Plantation, FL 33317

CHADD has local chapters nationwide and provides support to families of children with ADD and information to professionals. CHADD publishes a newsletter several times a year and holds an annual national conference on ADD.

National Attention Deficit Disorder Association
   (Nat'l ADDA)
1070 Rosewood, Suite A
Ann Arbor, MI 48104

National ADDA specializes in providing information to help adults and families with ADD to lead better and more successful lives. This organization founded the ADDA Adult Support Group Network and also holds a national conference on ADD.

Learning Disabilities Association (LDA)
4156 Library Road
Pittsburgh, PA 15234

LDA is a nonprofit organization, which has fifty state affiliates and more than 600 local chapters. LDA is concerned with finding and exploring solutions for many types of learning problems, including those that result from attention deficit disorder.

National Center for Learning Disabilities
381 Park Ave., South, Suite 1420
New York, NY 10016
This organization will mail information regarding various problems, including ADD, that young people face. Separate packages are put together for adults, children, and teachers.

National Information Center for Children and Youth
    with Disabilities
P.O. Box 1492
Washington, D.C. 20013-1492

This organization will mail information regarding various problems, including ADD, that young people face.

Orton Dyslexia Society
724 York Road
Baltimore, MD 21204

The Orton Dyslexia Society is concerned with the education of dyslexic students. It helps students receive proper education and training and also provides information about dyslexia to the general public.

GLOSSARY

antidepressant: a type of medication designed to ease depression, sometimes beneficial to people with attention deficit disorder

attention deficit disorder (ADD): a condition that involves several related symptoms that fall into three main categories: inattention, impulsiveness, and hyperactivity

behavior management: a type of treatment that focuses on changing problematic behavior and actions in everyday life

chronic: refers to a symptom or condition that generally develops slowly and persists for a long period of time, often for an entire lifetime

clonidine: a high-blood-pressure medication that is also sometimes effective in treating symptoms of attention deficit disorder

Cylert: a stimulant medication used in the treatment of attention deficit disorder

depression: an emotional state characterized by feelings of sadness, hopelessness, and worthlessness

Dexedrine: a stimulant medication used to treat the symptoms of attention deficit disorder

dyslexia: a language-communication disorder that affects one's ability to read, write, spell, and/or speak

hyperactivity: overactivity, or more activity than is considered normal; the inability to stay still when required to do so

impulsiveness: the tendency to act before thinking about the consequences

inattention: difficulty in concentrating on the task at hand or event in progress, especially over a long period of time

nervous system: the part of the body system that includes the brain, spinal cord, and nerves and that receives and transmits sensory information

neurologist: A medical doctor who specializes in treating problems of the nervous system

Norpramin: a tricyclic antidepressant medication also used to treat the symptoms of attention deficit disorder

pediatrician: a medical doctor who specializes in the care of children and adolescents

psychiatrist: a medical doctor who specializes in the treatment of mental, emotional, and/or behavioral disorders

psychologist: a professional who counsels people who have mental, emotional, and/or behavioral disorders

Ritalin: a stimulant medication used to treat the symptoms of attention deficit disorder

stimulant: a type of medication that is used to treat the symptoms of attention deficit disorder

therapist: a professional who works with children and adults to solve problems, discuss feelings, or change behavior. Psychiatrists, psychologists, and social workers are therapists

Tofranil: a tricyclic antidepressant medication also used to treat the symptoms of attention deficit disorder

tricyclic antidepressant: a type of medication used to treat depression and the symptoms of attention deficit disorder

FURTHER READING

For Children and Teenagers
Gehret, Jeanne. *Eagle Eyes: A Child's Guide to Paying Attention.* Fairport, NY: Verbal Images Press, 1991.

Gehret, Jeanne. *I'm Somebody Too.* Fairport, NY: Verbal Images Press, 1993.

Quinn, Patricia O. and Judith M. Stern. *Putting on the Brakes.* New York: Magination Press, 1991.

For Parents, Teachers, and Older Readers
Bain, Lisa J. *A Parent's Guide to Attention Deficit Disorders.* New York: Dell Publishing, 1991.

Fowler, Mary Cahill. *Maybe You Know My Kid: A Parent's Guide to Identifying, Understanding, and Helping Your Child with Attention-Deficit Hyperactivity Disorder.* Secaucus, NJ: Carol Publishing Group, 1990.

Garber, Stephen H., Marianne Daniels Garber, and Robyn Freedman Spizman. *If Your Child is Hyperactive, Inattentive, Impulsive, Distractible: Helping the ADD (Attention Deficit Disorder) Child.* New York: Villard Books, 1990.

Greenberg, Gregory S. and Wade F. Horn. *Attention Deficit Hyperactivity Disorder: Questions & Answers for Parents.* Champaign, IL: Research Press, 1991.

Hunsucker, Glenn. *Attention Deficit Disorder.* Abilene, TX: Forrest Publishing, 1988, revised 1993.

Ingersoll, Barbara D. and Sam Goldstein. *Attention Deficit Disorder and Learning Disabilities: Realities, Myths, and Controversial Treatments.* New York: Doubleday, 1993.

Wender, Paul H. *The Hyperactive Child, Adolescent, and Adult: Attention Deficit Disorder Through the Lifespan.* New York: Oxford University Press, 1987.

INDEX

DATE DUE

SEP 2 9 '97			
JAN 0 5 '98			
APR 1 7 '98	ILL: 1471282 PSm		
JUL 2 2 '98			
GAYLORD			PRINTED IN U.S.A